The Parkers of St James's

Miranda Comes To Town

published by
THORNEY ISLAND BOOKS

The Parkers of St James's

Miranda Comes To Town

words by
John McLaren

pictures by
Adam Relf

edited by
Alex Antscherl & Katharine McCallum

THORNEY ISLAND

Published by Thorney Island Books

First published 2012

Copyright © John McLaren
Illustrations copyright © Adam Relf
Design: Redcow Creative
Art direction: Clare Conway & Graham Ogilvie
Production management: Geoff Barlow

Set in Plantin and Snell
Printed and bound in China by WKT Co. Ltd

British Library Cataloguing in Publication Data

ISBN: 978-0-9571353-0-7

For the real Miranda,
with more love than words can express

acknowledgements

Of all the many kind people who have helped bring this book
to fruition, the greatest of all thanks are due to *Madeleine Milne* (of course),
Ken Grier, Marion Lloyd, Karen Mistry and Mark Searle.

So many others must also be acknowledged for their advice,
assistance, and kindness, including:

*Angelie Hosala, Maite Beltran, Moira Bennett, Wiltrud and Manfred Bischoff, Freya Booth,
Ning Ning Craven, Rachel and Mischa Damev, Marnie Dawson Carr, Fionnuala Duggan, Miriam and Andy Embury,
Jenni Enslow, Pat and David Gay, Justine and Bill Gower, Nikki Griffiths, Bounce and Bill Heald,
Lilian and Florian Hippe, Inge Hirsch, Sylvie and Bernard de Lattre, Nicola Leach,
Chris and Roger Lewis, Tracy Long, Joshua and Oliver Matovu, Dena and Gordon McCallum, Catherine McCauley,
Annabel McLaren, Margaret McLaren, Catherine Meyer, Peter Michael, Rosemary Milne, Elizabeth Mullings-Smith,
Anait and Zograb Nalbandian, Yasmin Pakzad, Rama, Hetal, Yogesh and Mutesh Patel,
Lesley and Peter Qvortrup, Caroline Roy, Heather and Hernan Sanchez, Sandy Scholey, Anne Smith,
Diane Stidham, Annabel Swan, Shirley Thompson, Elie Vannier and Sally Yap.*

Miranda's wonderful friends –

*Cecily Jones, Magdalena Adroher, Jacob Egan, Cyprus Egloff-Curran, Lok Hin Fan, Lyla Goddard,
Selina Haitsma Mulier, Alexia Ilic, Scarlett Laydon McCabe, Evangeline and Olivia Leech, Maud Lindsay,
Elena Maddocks, Bray Rudd, Sofia Russo, Carl Sternby, Allegra Stott, Theone Turton,
Julia Del Val Vecino, Alexander Van Den Berg, Chen Wang, Daisy and India Wolstenholme, and Felicia and Sophie Zirps.*

And her equally wonderful teachers

– at nursery school –
*Kay King, Marianne Bokmans, Lucinda Byron Evans, Katie Clark,
Polly Hewlett, Emily Snagge, C-J Strudwick, Trudy Twigg, and Nicole Watson.*

– and at big school –
Sebastian Hepher, Olivia Cartwright, Ellen Millar and Kelly Wailes.

*I*t was a stinking, rotten, ghastly, utterly miserable day in the park, so bad that St James himself would have been embarrassed about it. Even the mallards, moorhens and geese, who normally liked nothing better than being thoroughly wet, loathed the way the rain was slanting down into their eyes. It was so nasty that Ice and Cool, the young black swans, had for once stopped rapping, and Bigmouth, the pelican, had his head down so low his long baggy beak was poking out backwards between his legs.

As for squirrels Nutty and Amnesia, they just couldn't get comfortable. However much they scuttled around trying to get warm, or climbed trees trying to get dry, nothing worked. They would clamber along branches and choose big crackly brown leaves to shelter under, but as soon as they pulled these handy umbrellas down on top of their heads, the leaves always suddenly and mysteriously fell off.

They had to keep busy anyway – this was autumn, the season for them to gather nuts and hide them for the winter ahead. Nutty and Amnesia thought they made a very good team. Nutty was the expert at picking the best nuts, sorting them out by size and colour. Years of experience had taught him which colours tasted best and which sizes were easiest to carry.

Amnesia left that complicated stuff to Nutty. Her biggest contribution was to remember where they hid all the nuts. She was pretty sure she had done a good job last winter, but to tell the truth, it was such a long time ago, she couldn't recall.

What she *did* remember, though, was that today was a very important day. With one speedy flick of a paw, she brushed the rainwater from above her eyes and looked up towards Nutty. "I'm *so* excited," she said. "Today's the day she's coming – our red cousin from the country, Miranda."

Nutty nodded happily. "Do you think she'll be as pretty as everyone says?"

"I'm sure she will – maybe even more lovely," said Amnesia. "After all, they say her beauty is the talk of all Hampshire. Just think what fun we'll have showing her off, especially to the white swans – they usually think they're by far the most glamorous."

Nutty chuckled at the thought. "I bet they go as green as emeralds with envy."

Amnesia laughed too, but suddenly her expression grew more serious. "Don't forget, Nutty, however excited we get about showing her around, we must be very strict about keeping her on the north side. She's never been to London before, so she won't know the rules."

"We must teach her," said Nutty. "It would be *far* too dangerous for her to go near the south side." He shuddered at the thought. The south side of the park was where the scary, evil squirrels, Bashem and Slashem, ruled the roost. If Miranda ventured there she might fall into their clutches. All the birds and animals in the park were terrified of them. They were really nasty –

nipping, kicking, punching and generally bullying anyone who got in their way. And they were also horribly sneaky: only last week a group of longlegs had arrived, bringing bread to feed the ducks. Bashem and Slashem barged right in front and did cute little dances. The delighted longlegs fed and took photos of them instead. Squirrels don't even *like* bread – it was just Bashem and Slashem showing the ducks who was in charge.

It wasn't just birds that were terrorised by Bashem and Slashem. They were just as mean to other squirrels on the south side. Every week in winter, all those squirrels had to go to their hiding places and hand over one nut in ten to the dreadful duo – or else.

The evil squirrels themselves were very pleased with the way this worked. They didn't have to do any of that boring work gathering their own nuts, since they knew that the other squirrels would do this for them. Nor, since they weren't afraid of anyone, did they have to bother about hiding their stash in lots of different places, and instead they stored all the nuts in one very big hole high in the trunk of the biggest chestnut tree on the south side. With such an enormous supply of nuts to eat and getting no exercise collecting them, the pair grew fatter and fatter, which meant they couldn't run very fast, but then again, why would they ever need to? Running wasn't very dignified, and just walking slowly through their patch, rolling their big shoulders, was enough to terrify everyone.

The one silver lining in this very dark cloud was that, until now at least, the pair had kept entirely to the south side, probably because all the squirrels there already provided more nuts than they could eat. However, Nutty, Amnesia and all the other north-siders occasionally fretted that one day Bashem and Slashem would come over the bridge and set up the same racket in the north. But this was so horrible a prospect that, whenever possible, they put it out of their minds and thought about nicer things.

*T*oday, for example, having given up trying to keep dry and warm and accepting that he would be a cold, wet squirrel, Nutty had concentrated for what felt like ages on finding and sorting through nuts. He stopped, looked up, and cocked his head as he heard the chime of Big Ben. From the north side they could make out the tip of the famous tower, but the clock-face itself was hidden behind other buildings. If they had wanted to see it, they would have had to go to the south side, which of course was way too risky. So they had taught themselves to tell the time by listening out for the chimes.

Nutty waited patiently as the bells went through their *ding dong, ding dong, ding dong, ding dong* palaver before they got on to the more serious matter of striking the hour. He loved to play a guessing game with himself, trying to work out from little clues what time it might be. In this case, he was pretty sure it was late morning, perhaps eleven o'clock, or twelve at the latest. On a fine day, even in autumn, anywhere near lunchtime there would be the tell-tale signs of longlegs escaping from the stone and glass cages where they were forced to work, and sitting on the park benches to eat from their boxes or bags of longleg food. But not on a horrible day like this. Nutty was forced to admit he had no idea at all, and before he had any more time for even the wildest guess, the bells had stopped *ding dong*-ing and went *boom* – Nutty counted *one* carefully – *boom* – that was *two*. Nutty waited, confidently expecting a lot more chimes.

Amnesia was standing right beside him, listening too. She was pretty good up to three booms, but when the booms got to four, she usually forgot the first one. Then if there were five booms, she forgot not only the first but the second, and so on. This meant that, however many booms there were, Amnesia would always conclude that it was either one, two, or three o'clock. On most days this didn't matter an awful lot, but today it was a very important piece of information, because Miranda was due to arrive at two o'clock. So Nutty listened very hard indeed.

Amnesia looked over at him. "Have the booms stopped?"

"*Shhhhhh,*" replied Nutty tartly. "I'm concentrating."

Amnesia fell silent for a moment then glanced back across at Nutty. "Well, I make it two o'clock."

Nutty shook his head irritably. "When you make it two o'clock, it could be five o'clock, or eight, or eleven, or just about any o'clock."

Amnesia put her head to one side and scratched the top of it with her right paw. "I'm sure that only a few moments ago I knew there was something very important about two o'clock. I wish I could recall …"

"*Shhhh!*" said Nutty, very crossly this time.

Amnesia scratched again. "Whatever it is, I'm certain it's something very, very important."

Nutty was getting very fed up with her. "You are one scatty squirrel. I can't believe that you've forgotten already. I've reminded you ten times today. Now please be quiet and let me listen to the booms."

Amnesia pouted a little. She wasn't at all sure she liked being talked to this way. "Nutty, I may be scatty, but you are a particularly silly squirrel. Haven't you noticed that the booms have stopped? Now you've made me forget how many booms there were, but however many there were – that's the time!"

"*What?*" said Nutty. "There were only two. Can it really be two o'clock in the afternoon already? Then what are we doing? We should be at the north gate to welcome Miranda."

Amnesia put both of her paws to her mouth in horror. "*Great Squirrel-in-the-Sky!* What if she's already there and can't find us? It's all your fault for being so obsessed with nuts."

Nutty glared at her. "No it's not."

"*Tis.*"

"*Tisn't.*"

"*Tis.*"

"*Tisn't.*"

Their bickering was getting louder and louder and so furious that Amnesia had already forgotten what they were arguing about, when they were interrupted by a polite cough from behind them. But by now they were so excited about arguing that they altogether ignored it.

"*Tis.*"

"*Tisn't.*"

The coughing got louder too, until the whole thing settled into a steady rhythm of "tis, tisn't," cough, "tis, tisn't," cough, which soon sounded so musical that Amnesia began to dance around in a waltzy sort of way. Despite still being distinctly annoyed, Nutty couldn't stop his own musical instincts taking over, and he began jigging too. He went round and round, faster and faster, until his head started spinning and he tumbled right over, which stopped his "tisn't"-ing in its tracks. Amnesia, taken aback at seeing Nutty lying there, abruptly stopped her "tis"-ing too.

That just left the coughing sound, which carried on. For the first time, the two squirrels looked behind them to see where that sound was coming from, and got the biggest surprise. Who was this vision in red?

The vision spoke, in a very lovely, soft voice. "I'm so sorry – I didn't mean to startle you. I'm your cousin, Miranda. I arrived at the north gate a few minutes early. Instead of waiting, I asked directions from a friendly duck. He knew exactly who you are and where I could find you."

Amnesia smiled her broadest, warmest smile, stepped forward and gave Miranda an enormous hug. "Miranda! It's so good to meet you."

Miranda smiled too, but looked over with concern at Nutty, who was still clambering a little shakily to his feet. "Are you alright, sir?"

Nutty waved away his embarrassment with a flick of his tail. "Of course, of course. I simply slipped on the mud. It's lovely to see you, but we're not at all formal in this park. Please don't call me 'sir' – we're just Nutty and Amnesia."

But Miranda looked uncomfortable. "That's very friendly of you, but I couldn't possibly."

Amensia threw her furry head back in amusement at this young person's rural ways. "Why on earth not? Is it because we live so near to the Queen?"

"No, it's not that. It's because I was brought up to show respect to the elderly."

The smile vanished remarkably fast from Amnesia's face. "*Elderly?*" she said, her voice sounding more than a little annoyed.

Nutty wasn't sure whether to be amused or upset. "How old do you think we are, Miranda?"

"I don't know, sir, but my own mama and papa are very, very old, and they haven't turned at all grey yet, so you must be very, very, very old indeed."

Nutty and Amnesia looked at each other and laughed with relief. "Oh, is that it? It's because we're grey? Didn't you know we're a different species of squirrel? We were *born* grey."

Miranda would have blushed scarlet if she hadn't been so red already. "I'm *so* sorry. How can you ever forgive me?" But then she realised she was as puzzled as she was embarrassed. "But if we are different species, how can we be cousins?"

Nutty put on the air – which from time to time he was inclined to do –

of a senior school teacher. "Well, first of all, we're cousins twice or thrice removed. Which makes us quite distant cousins."

"Very distant," agreed Miranda. "Over seventy miles. It took me *weeks* to get here."

"That's not what that expression means," said Nutty, wishing he had a blackboard and chalk to draw a diagram. "But nevertheless, some of our relatives got married a long time ago and the groom was a red and the bride was a grey."

"Goodness me," said Miranda. "What colour were their children? Greyish red or reddish grey?"

"That was the odd thing," said Amnesia. "One was born grey and one completely red. You're descended from the red side, but, you never know, when you have a baby, it could pop out grey."

"*Chattering chestnuts!*" said Miranda, really quite taken aback by that idea.

Amnesia came forward and put a cousinly paw on her shoulder. "Let's forget all about colours – you're family and that's all that matters. Now, you must be famished. Come and have a nibble."

"Thank you very much, Amnesia, but I'd rather go and see Buckingham Palace right away."

"Not today, surely? It'll be dark before long, and maybe tomorrow the weather will be better."

"But it won't be dark for a little while yet. Can't I just have a quick peek?"

"Very well," said Amnesia, "we'll show you the way."

They set off. Amnesia and Nutty didn't choose the most direct route, because they were just as excited about showing Miranda off to other Parkers as she was to see the palace, so they went a slightly roundabout way, to make sure they bumped into some of their friends.

The first to come within sight was Ning Ning, the mandarin duck. Being a female, her coat wasn't quite as spectacular as the males', but nonetheless she was really very attractive, and in truth Nutty had a teeny bit of a crush on her. I don't have to tell you that it is very rare for a squirrel to have a crush on a duck – indeed Amnesia considered this distinctly odd. When Ning Ning saw Miranda between the two grey squirrels, she waddled rapidly towards them and opened her beak with a flourish.

"Ga-ga."

Nutty beamed and whispered to Miranda. "Ga-ga is quack-quack in Chinese."

"Or so she says," muttered Amnesia.

"Shhh," hissed Nutty, "she'll hear you." Then he spoke up. "Hello, Ning Ning. May I introduce our cousin from Hampshire, Miranda?"

"How do you do, Miranda," said Ning Ning.

"Good afternoon, Ning Ning. Did you really come all the way from China?"

"Not … personally," admitted Ning Ning, her crest a little fallen, "but my grandparents – or maybe *their* grandparents – did, and we've maintained our language and culture ever since. Indeed, we still have our own very small Chinatown."

"A Chinatown – here in London? How very exotic! I'd love to come and see it."

Ning Ning looked delighted. "Please come tomorrow. Our Chinatown is opposite Horse Guards Parade. It's only three hundred metres from here. We serve real Chinese food."

Nutty grinned broadly. "Will there be rice quackers?" Ning Ning smiled politely – Nutty must have used that line to her about a million times before. This didn't stop him bouncing about with amusement, and his face lit up when he thought of another good line. "Do you like it when I quack jokes?"

Miranda didn't quite get Nutty's jokes, and became even more confused when he slid down to the ground and began rolling to and fro, clutching his sides, with tears streaming down his face. Amnesia was chuckling too. She was the perfect audience for Nutty's jokes because, as far she was aware, she had never heard any of them before, despite the fact that he only had a repertoire of about six or seven, and he used most of them every day.

Ning Ning politely changed the subject. "Miranda, that's a very lovely coat you have. I didn't know you could get those in red."

Miranda returned the compliment immediately. "Your down looks so silky – such high quality. And I love your eye stripes."

"Thank you," beamed Ning Ning, delighted that Miranda had noticed. First impressions were so important. Normally Ning Ning preferred to be introduced to new friends when it was sunny and the bright light showed off her multi-coloured tail feathers to the greatest advantage.

By now Nutty had almost stopped laughing and was getting up and wiping away his tears. "OK then, I suppose we'd better get on."

Ning Ning smiled. "See you all in Chinatown tomorrow."

As Ning Ning waddled off, the squirrels saw the white swans gliding up the lake. Although they were trying hard to avoid the impression of being at all curious, Amnesia spotted them change course quite deliberately and steer close to the bank. Amnesia called out, "Hello, Bianca. Hi, Blanche. How are you both?"

The white swans never spoke, but their command of gestures was very advanced. They both bowed their long necks gracefully in greeting.

"This is our cousin, Miranda. Don't you think she's lovely?"

Bianca and Blanche glanced at each other, by way of consultation, then nodded discreetly. Nutty knew enough about handling the swans to know that you always had to throw in a little flattery. "Of course, she could never be as elegant as you two, but for a squirrel, we think she's tops."

Like synchronised swimmers, both swans turned their heads ever so slightly to one side, in happy acknowledgement of the compliment. Although they didn't have the words to say it, they certainly thought that Miranda was by far the most beautiful squirrel they had ever seen. Privately they had long shared the view that all the squirrels in the park looked positively dowdy and had agreed with each other that, if they were squirrels, they would immediately dye their coats some more fashionable colour – a nice shade of white, perhaps.

As Bianca and Blanche looked towards the far side of the lake, they could see Cool and Ice approaching. Bianca and Blanche didn't really approve of these youngsters – they considered them far too noisy and energetic. Instead of simply gliding around, the pair were forever rapping and jiving in the most unswanly manner. The white swans always tried to keep well away from them, so they quickly nodded goodbye to the three squirrels and glided away before the black swans arrived.

However, Nutty and Amnesia liked all the swans equally, and so smiled warmly as Cool and Ice sailed up. Cool went immediately into a rap, his wing-tips jabbing the air with the beat.

"Howdy, Am. Howdy, Nut,
  Glad to see you're not sitting down on your butts.
  Ice and me, we find it a pain,
  These lousy grey skies and filthy rain."

Ice, wings jabbing too, quickly took up the refrain.

"Looks like a stranger you brought along with you,
  You could introduce her, if you wanted to.
  Though we know the Regent Rowdies and the Hyde Park Mob,
  We've never seen a squirrel with such a smart paint job."

Amnesia grinned proudly. "This is our cousin, Miranda. She does have a fetching colour, doesn't she?"

Cool, jabbing and swaying more than ever, came right back.

"We're straight-talking swans, so we'll cut to the chase,
  Your cuz is cute, fit, and totally ace.
  Can't recall when dull St James
  Saw a bit of glam like this beautiful dame."

Ice was, if anything, outswaying him and joined in again.

"Welcome, Miss Miranda, good to have you here,
  Hope you'll come out with us for a couple of beers.
  We dance real good, and jive real fine,
  We can sure show you one heck of a time."

Nutty held up a paw. "That's a very nice invitation, fellas. Miranda will have a very full social diary while she's here, but of course she'll bear in mind your kind offer."

Miranda was more concerned about all the time they were spending chatting, and looked up at the sky, which was beginning to darken a little. Nutty saw this and took the hint. "Cool, Ice, we must be getting on. See you later."

The black swans each held out their right wing-tips for the three squirrels to punch in a brotherly way, turned and glided off, still rapping.

"Well done, Bro, we made our mark,
  Now she knows we're dudes, the kings of the park ..."

The next lines were lost as the black swans moved further away. Watching them go, Miranda turned to Nutty. "They seemed very friendly, but do they really drink beer?"

Nutty smiled. "Oh, I don't suppose so, but they probably wouldn't feel very cool inviting you for a few sips of rainwater … Oh dear, here comes Bigmouth. If you start chatting with the pelicans, you never can get away. They're such *gossips*. That's why they evolved those big beaks – to hold all the chit-chat."

As Bigmouth came up to them, Nutty held a paw up firmly. "Sorry, Bigmouth, can't talk now. We're in a screaming hurry."

Bigmouth hung his head sadly. "I only wanted to say hello to your glamorous cousin. Everyone's talking about her, and it seems half the Parkers have already been introduced. I feel very left out."

Amnesia felt rather sorry for him. In truth, she was quite keen on a little gossip herself and Bigmouth always knew what scandals were brewing. "Tell you what, Bigmouth – why don't you drop by for tea tomorrow? I'll see if I can get one of the mallards to catch something and I'll bake a fishcake. Then you can bring us up to date with all the latest."

"Thank you," said Bigmouth, brightening noticeably.

So they said goodbye to him, walked on, and five minutes later finally arrived at the west end, at the edge of the road which marked the border between the park and the palace. Although neither liked to admit it, Nutty and Amnesia were both terrified of crossing the road. There were always brightly coloured, unpleasantly noisy metal boxes whizzing to and fro on

the road. Sometimes the boxes suddenly stopped to let longlegs cross, and sometimes they drove very fast right past where the longlegs were standing. There seemed no rhyme or reason to it. Within the park, everything was clear. If a pelican came anywhere near a crow, for example, the crow got out of its way. In the same way, if a longleg let a dog off its rope, the squirrels made themselves scarce, usually shinning up the nearest tree. However, the longlegs and the metal boxes never seemed to be able to decide who was boss, hence all this starting and stopping confusion, which made it very difficult indeed for any passing squirrel to work out when to hang back and when to dash across the road.

Nutty had suffered several very close shaves, and Amnesia had endured one particularly traumatic incident when, halfway across the road, she forgot why she was crossing, so turned round to go back, then in a flash remembered the reason and spun back in the original direction, somehow prompting the most terrifying screeching and honking from boxes all around her. The scare had put years on her, and privately Amnesia blamed it for the small shock of white fur on the top of her head, which, when Nutty wasn't looking, she had recently started to cover up by rubbing in a touch of greyish mud.

"Shall we escort you across?" asked Nutty gallantly, if a little hesitantly.

"Oh no, please don't bother. I can manage very well on my own, thank you," replied Miranda.

"Are you really, really sure?" said Amnesia, looking ever so slightly relieved. "But of course we'll wait for you right here. Make sure you're back well before dark. Whatever you do, don't go to the south side. And if you happen to notice two exceptionally large, hideously ugly squirrels while you're at the palace, keep well away from them. They're called Bashem and Slashem and they're mad, bad, and dangerous to know."

Miranda nodded obediently, but Amnesia wasn't finished yet. "We also need to teach you something about protocol."

"What's that?" asked Miranda, who had never heard that word before.

"It's something you'll never need in Hampshire," said Nutty, puffing out his furry chest proudly, "but it's terribly important for those of us who live in London."

"Protocol means knowing what to do if you meet a member of the Royal Family," explained Amnesia. "First of all you have to curtsey, making sure you don't lose your balance and topple over, which would be very undignified. Then you must remember to call the Queen by her real name, which is 'Majesty'. Rather confusingly, the others are all called 'Royal Highness'."

"Is that because they're very tall?" guessed Miranda.

"Absolutely!" replied Nutty, impressed by how clever their cousin was.

"But what about the little children? Are they called 'Royal Lowness'?"

"Of course not!" laughed Nutty. "They're called 'Royal Shortness'."

"Well, thank you for teaching me about protocol, and I do promise to steer well clear of Bashem and Slashem," said Miranda. "Now, I'd better be off." And, spotting a tiny gap, she suddenly darted into the road, right in the path of the roaring, speeding metal boxes with their scary blazing lights. Nutty's heart jumped right into his mouth and Amnesia couldn't bear to watch. But when she opened her eyes she was delighted to see that Miranda had somehow managed to dodge safely through the traffic. They both breathed huge sighs of relief and settled down to wait patiently for her return.

*M*iranda got terrifically excited looking at the fine, tall, broad building with its golden gates and the guards in their smart uniforms and gigantic black hats. She wondered what the rooms inside were like – they must surely be some of the biggest in the world, maybe filled with great big piles of gold, silver, diamonds, emeralds and rubies. She spent so much time thinking about it that she altogether failed to notice how much time was passing and how dark the sky was becoming. By the time she looked up, it was nearly pitch black. She realised she couldn't remember exactly where she'd crossed the road, and that meant she wasn't so sure she could find the place where her cousins were waiting. To make matters worse, the rain was falling harder than ever, and when she got to the side of the road, the combination of the raindrops falling from her eyelids into her eyes and the dazzling lights of the metal boxes was making it far more difficult to spot a big enough gap to cross safely.

For ten or fifteen minutes she just stood there, growing less and less confident. Once or twice she stepped a metre into the road and froze, terrified, when she realised, almost too late, that the metal boxes were coming at her far faster than she thought. In other circumstances she might have slipped under the palace gates and found somewhere to curl up until it was light again, but she knew that if she didn't return, Amnesia and Nutty would worry terribly. But what could she do? Should she just close her eyes and make a blind run for it?

Just at that moment she heard a deep voice behind her. "You got a problem, kid?" Miranda turned round and gasped. Only inches away and towering above her were two of the biggest squirrels she had ever seen.

"I'm trying to get across, but it's not very easy."

The other squirrel spoke up, his voice even deeper than the first. "You visiting someone in the park, kid?"

"Yes. I'm Nutty and Amnesia's cousin."

"Oh yeah?" said the first big squirrel, smirking. "Only way you can be their cousin is if you fell in a pot of red paint."

"We're very distant cousins. They're waiting for me on the north side."

The big squirrels whispered to each other, then the second one spoke up. "It's your lucky day, kid. You happen to have run into the two most helpful squirrels in the park. We'll help you across."

"That's very kind of you," said Miranda gratefully.

And with that, the two squirrels grabbed Miranda by one arm each, lifted her clean off the ground, and in a blur of furry tails they were safely across the road.

"Thank you very much. You can put me down now."

"That wouldn't be a good idea," said the first squirrel. "With all this rain, it's very muddy. You wouldn't want to get your dainty little red feet dirty now, would you?"

"I'm used to mud, and I'm very good at cleaning my feet."

"It's not just the mud you have to think about," said the second squirrel. "If you're not careful, you can step in goose poo. Man, is that smelly and slimy! Stinks your feet out for days. No, it'll be much better for you if we carry you all the way back to your cousins."

Before Miranda could protest any more, they strode off. Even when she wriggled, she realised she was powerless to resist. She looked up and noticed they were veering to the right. "Are we going the correct way? Isn't the north side to the left? I'm sure that's the way I came."

"You're mistaken, kid. But I can't see your cousins anywhere. Maybe they got fed up waiting for you and went back home. Why don't we take you there instead?"

"No, no. I'm sure they're still waiting."

However, the two big squirrels ignored her and set off again. Miranda began to have a very bad feeling in the pit of her stomach. Desperately she tried to see if she could work out for herself which way was north and south. In daylight it would have been easy, because her parents had made her learn that the sun rises in the east and sets in the west. Throughout her long journey to London she had only travelled by day, so the sun had been her guide. What was she to do now that there was no light left at all in the sky?

The deeper they walked into the park, the more alarmed she became. Nothing looked familiar. She glanced sideways and for the first time noticed that both of the big squirrels had marks like tattoos on their chests. One looked like it was a 'B' and the other resembled an 'S'. That gave her a very worrying thought. She might be in very big trouble indeed.

"What are your names? Do they begin with 'B' and 'S'?"

The big squirrels glanced down at their own chests. This kid was no fool. "Yeah . . ." said the first squirrel. "I'm called . . . er . . . um . . . Benny, and this is my twin brother, Sam."

Miranda looked warily into his eyes. "So you're definitely not called Bashem and Slashem?"

"Certainly not," said the second big squirrel. "You'd be very unlucky

It was very tasty. As she nibbled on, she watched as one of the big squirrels poked the fire with a stick. It burned more brightly than ever as the flames jumped higher. Miranda carefully put the half-nibbled acorn back on the pile and stood up.

"Thank you. I feel much better now, but I must be getting along." As she stepped forward, one of the squirrels stuck out a huge fat haunch, blocking her way altogether.

"You ain't going anywhere, kid. Sit down."

Miranda had no choice but to do as she was told. Now she was sure of the truth, and bravely spoke up. "I don't believe you're called Benny and Sam at all."

"Yeah? So what are we called?"

"I think you're Bashem and Slashem."

"So what if we are? What are you going to do about it? Make a run for it? Go on, punk, make our day."

The squirrels chuckled to each other.

"Watch out, Slashem. Maybe she'll beat us up."

"You could be right, Bashem, look at the size of her muscles, ha ha."

Miranda began shivering, and then shivered more and more until she began shaking, but her voice was still steady. "Why have you brought me here? What are you going to do with me?"

Bashem smiled thinly. "See this fire? We could roast you alive over it."

Miranda gulped. Now she was not so much shaking as quaking. "But why would you do that? Squirrels don't eat squirrels. We don't eat any sort of meat, in fact."

"*We* do – if we feel like it," boasted Slashem. "Or we might roast you just for fun – and then feed you to the dogs in the morning."

"But I don't want to be eaten by dogs," pleaded Miranda. For all her bravery, now there were tears forming in the corners of her eyes, which only made the cruel Slashem and Bashem grin more.

"But before we roast you, we'll first give that dumb Nutty and that daft Amnesia the chance to ransom you."

"*Ransom* me?"

"Yeah, kid, you've been squirrelnapped. Your cousins will have to pay richly to get you back. We've been planning for ages to make a move on the north and you've given us the perfect opportunity. Now come here."

Bashem began moving towards her. Miranda shrank back as far as she could, until she couldn't shrink any further and was pressing herself hard against the nut-pile. It was no good though. Bashem stepped forward, reached out with one big, fat paw, grabbed hold of her and dragged her to him.

Miranda struggled fiercely but vainly. While Bashem held her in his iron grasp, Slashem took hold of her tail and yanked and yanked until a whole big pawful of red fur came away. Then Bashem let her go, and she scampered back towards the nut-pile, but oh, oh, oh, how her tail hurt! It was too sore to sit on.

She watched as Slashem picked up an empty nutcase and stuffed all the red fur into it. He handed it to Bashem, who went to the mouth of the hole and waited for a few seconds until he saw a Canada goose sauntering nearby.

"*Oi*, Birdbrain. Yeah, *you*."

The poor goose – whose real name was Rockie – jumped halfway out of his feathers. He obediently waddled across until he stood right below the hole.

"You know Nutty and Amnesia – over on the north side?"

"Sure I do."

"OK – take this to them." Bashem threw the nut down and the goose picked it up in his beak. "When you get there, tell those two stupid squirrels that what's in that nut is proof we've got their redhead cousin."

Rockie nodded. Bashem carried on. "We want all the nuts they've hidden for winter."

Rockie dropped the nut in surprise and disbelief. "*All* their nuts? That means they'll starve."

Bashem just smiled. "Tough – unless they bring us at least a hundred within the hour, the red is dead. Better get moving, Birdbrain, the clock's ticking. And we want *you* to guide them here personally."

But, apart from Nutty and Amnesia, almost everyone was staring down at the ground. They weren't natural heroes. Even Cool and Ice, who normally liked to act tough, were looking far from warlike.

Nutty sighed. "Thanks, Rockie, but I don't think that'll work. I think we'd better get on with gathering nuts."

But then a small voice spoke up. "*No way!*"

Everyone looked around to see who had spoken. They were all astonished to see it was Ning Ning. She stood up and stepped right into the middle of the circle, a stern look on her face.

"You lot may be afraid of those bad squirrels, but *I'm* not. I'm with Rockie."

There was a general groan. What could a pint-sized bundle of feathers do about a dire situation like this? It was just big talk – and the time for talking was over.

Nutty was the only one who was willing to give her the benefit of the doubt. Indeed, the way she was standing there, not looking at all scared was actually rather impressive – not to mention attractive. "Hold on. Let her have her say. Go on, Ning Ning."

"Thank you, Nutty. Before I begin, I'm quite well aware of what you all say behind my back – especially you, Bigmouth." The pelican had the decency to look slightly embarrassed. Ning Ning gave him the eye as his face slowly turned from white to pink and then to crimson. Ning Ning scanned the rest of the group. "You all think I'm not really Chinese. Well, not only can I quack perfectly fluently, I have one other Chinese talent none of you know about. See my black stripes?" And she indicated the strong black lines which sat between the blues and the whites of her handsome tail feathers.

"I was given these when I got my kung-fu black belt. Wanna see my moves?"

And to everyone's surprise, in a blur of motion she executed an astonishing series of jabs, kicks and beak thrusts. They had never seen anything like it. When Ning Ning started speaking again, they were all ears.

"Now, I'm willing to take on one or even both of those squirrels, but I have a problem. Rockie, how high is the hole?"

"Oh, it's quite high – about twice my height, I guess."

"Which makes it like ten times yours." said one mallard to Ning Ning.

"More like twelve, if you ask me," said another. Mallards were notorious for being better at mathematics than tact.

Ning Ning scowled furiously at them both before returning to Rockie. "So, what's the deal? Any chance we can taunt them into coming down to fight?"

Rockie wiggled his head from side to side as he pondered. "We could try, I suppose, but they would probably see through it. They're not stupid, those two. They won't risk leaving Miranda unguarded."

Ning Ning looked stumped. "So if they won't come out and fight, how can I get in there?"

Suddenly Rockie started jumping up and down with excitement. "Ning Ning, you've just made me think of a plan. And, although I say it myself, it's an absolute humdinger. But it all depends on you, Bigmouth!"

"*Me?*" gulped Bigmouth.

"Yes, how brave are you feeling?"

"Not enormously," admitted Bigmouth.

It was Amnesia who quickly figured out how to give Bigmouth courage. "Just imagine if you helped Ning Ning and Rockie rescue Miranda. You'd be able to tell *everyone* all about it."

"That's true, I suppose," said Bigmouth, still a little uncertainly.

"Good. That's settled," said Rockie before Bigmouth could change his mind. "Nutty, you'll have to come too."

"Of course," said Nutty gamely. "There's nothing I wouldn't do for Miranda." He nearly added "And for you too, Ning Ning," but he stopped himself just in time.

Next Rockie caught Cool's eye. "We need you and Ice too."

Cool and Ice looked at each other in consternation, prompting Ice to start up.

"We are tough and we are strong,
 We're both in favour of righting wrong.
 But surely it's cool to stay this side of the park,
 Particularly on nights when it's exceptionally dark."

Cool nodded in agreement.

"My bro is right, and he's pretty smart.
 However keen we are on taking part,
 Mama would be mad if we got caught,
 So it's best if we offer just moral support."

Nutty looked sternly at them. "If you two refuse to help, no one will ever consider you cool again. Not only that – the parliament might ban rapping altogether."

Bianca raised her beak snootily and looked over at them in a very superior fashion. It was exactly as she and Blanche had suspected – their tough act was all show.

Ice noticed Bianca's look; there was nothing that got his goat like a snooty swan. Boy, would he show her! Before he knew what he was doing, he had puffed out his chest and walked proudly over to join Ning Ning and Rockie.

Cool was horrified – he couldn't believe what Ice had just done. Now all eyes turned towards him. He stared back defiantly. "Look as much as you like," he muttered under his breath. No way was he going to be dumb enough to follow suit. But as everyone kept on staring, somehow he felt his precious cool beginning to drain away. Damn Ice and damn that Bianca, he thought, and with the deepest of sighs, stepped forward too.

"Thank you, Cool," said Nutty. "So, Rockie, tell us – what *is* the plan?"

"I'll tell you as we march over – there's no time now. What I need most is for each of the squirrels to bring two or three nuts. About twenty should be enough."

Amnesia was puzzled. What use was twenty? The bad squirrels were demanding at least a hundred. She feared horribly for Miranda. What if Rockie's plan didn't work?"

But she had very little time to dwell on her doubts.

In a trice, twenty nuts had been collected, and the little army marched off, with Rockie leading the way, followed by Bigmouth, who was quiet for once. Next came Nutty, then Ice and Cool, who were rapping in a rather subdued manner, and finally Ning Ning, who was waddling backwards, which is an extremely hard thing to do, in order to guard against any sneak attack from the rear.

As they reached the bridge across the lake, they all hesitated for a moment.

Rockie turned impatiently. "Come on, guys, we have to get on. The hour's nearly up."

"You're right," said Nutty, taking a very deep breath. "Let's do or die."

*I*nside the hole, Slashem threw another nutcase on the fire and sat back down. "Time's nearly up. You think those squirrels are coming?"

"They better be," said Bashem, as he threw a nasty glance over towards Miranda. "Or the redhead loses a lot more fur."

"Why don't we pull one of her ears off?"

"Yeah, that sounds a good game."

Poor Miranda, who had curled up in a ball on the floor of the hole, tried her best to ignore this new threat. Seconds later, she heard what sounded like Nutty's voice coming from below. She sprung up, hoping that salvation was near. Both bad squirrels jumped up too. Bashem said, "Must be them – let's go and see."

The hole was only big enough for one of those very large squirrels to look, so they shoved and jostled until Slashem won the jostling game and stuck his head out. He laughed out loud when he saw the little delegation. There was Nutty, with those two ridiculous black swans on one side of him, and on the other side, Rockie, plus one of the pelicans with a very bulging beak.

With suitable disdain in his voice, Slashem spoke to him. "Glad to see you saw sense. Where are the nuts?"

Nutty looked up. "We don't have a bag, and we couldn't think of another way to carry them, so Bigmouth brought them here in his beak."

"Oh yeah?" said Slashem. "Show me. Open the beak."

Nutty gestured to Bigmouth, who raised his beak up towards the hole and opened it a few inches. Despite the dark, Slashem could make out the unmistakeable shape of nuts.

"Good. How many are in there?"

"A hundred and five," said Nutty.

"You counted them yourself?"

"I did."

"You better have counted well, because if you're even one short, we'll be breakfasting on sautéed squirrel."

"They're there all right. Now, if you and Bashem would like to come down and bring Miranda, we'll hand them over."

Slashem shook his head. "No dice, Nutty. We don't trust you. We want them up here."

"But we've no way to get them up there. Unless ..."

"Unless what?" asked Slashem warily.

"Well, I suppose if Bigmouth stood on Rockie's back and raised his beak as high as he can, you could maybe reach in and take the nuts out."

"OK, let's try it," said Slashem, "but you don't get the redhead till we've counted out all hundred and five."

Nutty breathed a sigh of relief. It looked like Slashem had taken the bait. Could Rockie's crazy plan actually work?

Rockie lowered his head, and Bigmouth tried to hop up on his back. It took two or three hops before he made it, and even then he swayed rather unsteadily. Pelicans are not built for gymnastics. Once Bigmouth was up, Rockie waddled forward towards the tree. Wow, he thought, Bigmouth is one heavy pelican.

When they were in position, Bigmouth gingerly raised his beak until it was touching the bottom of the hole.

"OK," said Slashem, "open up. I'll pass them to Bashem."

Slowly Bigmouth opened his beak wide, and Slashem reached in. With gravity the nuts had all fallen to the back of the beak, so he had to reach in up to his shoulder before he felt the first nut. He pulled it out.

"One." He handed it behind him and they all heard Bashem repeating the count. He reached in again.

"Two." It felt like he had to go in even deeper before he got the third one.

"Three."

Bigmouth was beginning to find it a strain to keep his mouth so far open, and was willing Slashem to get a move on, but the fat squirrel was in no hurry.

"Four … Five … Six."

By the time he was reaching for the tenth, eleventh and twelfth nuts, Slashem had both shoulders in, and that was making Bigmouth feel decidedly nauseous. He tried hard to put it out of his mind – it would be a disaster if he was sick.

Down below, Rockie was suffering too, sweating heavily with the exertion. "Hang on, Rockie," exhorted Nutty. "Not much longer now."

But it took another three full minutes before Slashem called out "nineteen" and then "twenty". When he reached in again, he couldn't at first feel any nuts at all. But that was strange, because whenever he checked the outside of the beak, it was still bulging. The nuts must be even deeper inside. There was nothing for it but to put his head in too and have a proper look.

The whole pile that Bashem had made, after Slashem took them from Bigmouth's beak, went hurtling through the air, slamming into their faces and bodies, knocking them both clean off their feet. Ning Ning dashed to the mouth of the hole.

Beneath her, Nutty yelled out. "Fly, Ning Ning, fly."

"I can't," cried Ning Ning. "I've never learnt."

It was Rockie who saw the solution. "Bigmouth, open your beak, as wide as you can."

Bigmouth immediately did as he was bidden.

"Quick, Ning Ning, jump," called out Rockie.

Ning Ning looked down, then behind her. The squirrels were clambering back to their feet and heading her way. The fall still might kill her – or Bigmouth – but there was nothing else for it.

"*Whoooooo,*" screamed Ning Ning as she plummeted down, toppling forwards as she fell. For a horrible split-second they all thought she was going to miss the beak altogether, but clever old Bigmouth managed to move smartly to the side and catch her.

"*Gluuuuuuuubuuuuuu,*" was all the noise that came from Bigmouth. The impact had bruised the poor pelican's throat. Ning Ning was half knocked out too. Coughing and spluttering, Bigmouth lowered his beak and let her out on to the ground. Ning Ning tumbled out, and got to her feet.

Nutty looked delighted, but if he thought it was over, he was wrong. Up above him at the hole appeared a very, very, very angry-looking Bashem, glaring down at him.

Nutty turned to his side and hissed, "Ning Ning, Rockie, Bigmouth – you've done your stuff. Time you made yourselves scarce – get back to our place and tell Amnesia what's going on."

Ning Ning was reluctant to leave, but the other two birds dragged her away. Next, Nutty turned to Ice and Cool. "Guys, Miranda and I need to skedaddle, and we need a head start. Can you try to hold them up for a while? Flap your wings for all they're worth."

Ice nodded gravely.

"As for your plan, we're still at a loss,
  But we'll do what you say, because you is da boss."

He had no more than got the rap out when he and Cool had to leap straight into action. Slashem and Bashem were racing down the tree trunk and coming menacingly towards them. Ice and Cool advanced, spreading their big black wings, raising their heads to their full height. Now that battle was truly being joined, Cool was surprising himself by how little fear he felt. He eyeballed Bashem.

"Because you're big and fat, you think that you're tough,
  But we're here to tell you that ain't enough.
  You think you're the masters, but that's all lies;
  You're only chubby rodents wearing XL size."

The vengeful squirrels could hardly believe their luck. Nutty had done a bunk, but the daft redhead was rooted to the spot, less than fifty metres away. She was toast.

They lumbered forward, breathing heavily after all their exertions with the pesky black swans. It had been a while since they had run anywhere, and after a few more paces they were already puffing. But it was OK – the redhead was standing stock-still. She must be paralysed with fear. In the last few minutes their world had been shaken a little, but if they caught her, they could get their own back not only on her, but on all those impudent rascals who had dared to mess with them. Boy, would they pay!

They were within ten metres now, then eight, seven, six, five, four, three, two ... Bashem leapt through the air, determined to be the one to get hold of her first, but to his shock and displeasure, he hit the ground hard, clutching no more than thin air. She must have moved out of his reach at the very last second.

Slashem ran further forward towards where Miranda had stopped once again and, when he was within inches, he lunged headlong too – with exactly the same result. Furious, he got back to his feet, only to observe Bashem do the same all over again. For the next few minutes, this was repeated time after time. The redhead kept moving within range, and then whenever they leapt at her, somehow she managed to step clear. It made them madder and madder – so mad that they hardly noticed that they were now panting laboriously and their movements were getting less and less co-ordinated.

They were almost relieved when the redhead changed tactics, stopped the cat-and-mouse game, and ran away from them, settling into a steady trot. Although it was hard going, they were sure they would outlast her – being so young, and with such skinny legs, surely she wouldn't be able to keep this up.

But she surprised them, not only with her pace, but her direction. She was making no effort to head towards the bridge, and seemed instead to be happy going due east across the south side. Pretty soon they had reached the very east end, but instead of fleeing out of the park altogether, she simply turned round, easily evading their clumsy attempts at catching her, and headed back west. They barely noticed that she was leading them on a full tour of their patch, the territory where their word was law.

As the chase carried on, more and more birds and animals were observing the spectacle. Large numbers of mallards, moorhens, coots, teal and geese were quickly waddling closer for a better view. Squirrel after squirrel scampered down trees and raced across the grass to get nearer. Some hopped onto railings and used them as a sort of grandstand. But they couldn't work out what was going on. Why were Bashem and Slashem, who normally made a great point of strolling everywhere, so furiously chasing a red squirrel? And why wasn't that little squirrel looking scared? On the contrary, she almost looked like she was grinning. What on *earth* was going on? Whatever it was, something remarkable was happening, and the authority of the evil squirrels was rapidly vanishing.

"Totally," said Miranda very confidently.

"*Really?*" said Nutty for a third time.

Miranda just nodded, but with an exceedingly reassuring smile.

"Well, in that case I must say your mama sounds a very lovely squirrel and it would be an honour to meet her some day. Thank you very much, Miranda."

Feeling a great deal better, Nutty put more of a spring in his step. "Let's hurry up and get back. They'll all be ready to celebrate till dawn. You'll find Parkers know how to party. We can never get Ice and Cool off the dance floor. Bigmouth and Rockie just love to boogie, and the white swans are wonderful waltzers. Plus, you ain't seen nothing till you've seen Ning Ning do the twist!"

What with all the anxiety of being kidnapped, plus the excitement of the chase, not to mention her long journey from the country, Miranda was beginning to feel just a teeny bit weary. In any other circumstances, she wouldn't have minded curling up on her own for a little quiet time. However, she could see that this wasn't any old circumstance. And if there was going to be a party, she would have to pull out the stops to keep Hampshire's end up.

Spurred on by that thought, she bounded ahead even faster, so fast that soon Nutty was panting to keep up. Without warning he screeched to a halt. Miranda stopped too, and turned to see Nutty sniffing the air and glancing up towards the sky. "Look, it's stopped raining. Maybe it'll be a better day tomorrow – you can go back to Buckingham Palace."

"Thanks very much, Nutty," said Miranda with a wry grin, "but I don't think I'll bother." They both laughed. "Anyway," added Miranda, "we haven't got time to think about that now. If I'm not mistaken, it's nearly dawn already. So let's get to the party. Race you. Last one back's a longleg!"

And off they set, with Miranda at first in the lead, then Nutty straining every one of his little muscles to catch up. They were neck and neck when they stopped right in front of the welcoming group. As Miranda raised her right paw in salute, she felt her heart suddenly filling to overflowing with gratitude and affection. Although she had been there less than one whole day, she already knew that the bravest, the kindest, the very best of friends any squirrel could have were the Parkers of St James's.

The End

John McLaren began his career in the British diplomatic service, and then moved to investment banking and venture capital in Asia, the US and Europe. His first novel, *Press Send*, was published in 1997 and he has subsequently written four more – *Seventh Sense*, *Black Cabs*, *Running Rings* and *Blind Eye*, all published by Simon & Schuster. *The Parkers of St James's* is his first book for children.

Adam Relf studied illustration at Kingston University. Soon after graduating, he started work as a concept artist, working for various digital media and games companies. During this time, he began writing and illustrating children's books and had several published, including: *Arlo Makes a Friend*, *The Biggest Bear*, *Just Like Me*, *Sharks*, and *One Little Sheep*. Since then he has worked on an eclectic range of major projects. His adaptable style has allowed him to work in many areas, ranging from editorial, advertising and packaging design to games industry work.

He was born in London and, apart from a brief stint in Kent, has continued to live and work there. When not working, he enjoys tea, trees, old buildings, science, music, nature ... and feeding squirrels!